True Hearts Day Spellebration!

Adapted by Perdita Finn

Based on the screenplay written by George Doty IV

LITTLE, BROWN & COMPANY

LB kids

Little, Brown and Company

Hachette Book Group
1290 Avenue of the Americas, New York, NY 10104
Visit us at lb-kids.com

LB kids is an imprint of Little, Brown and Company.
The LB kids name and logo are trademarks of Hachette Book Group, Inc.

The publisher is not responsible for websites (or their content) that are not owned by the publisher.

First Edition: December 2016

ISBN 978-0-316-55143-4

Library of Congress Control Number: 2016943584

10 9 8 7 6 5 4 3 2 1

CW
Printed in the United States of America

Spring was in the air—and C.A. Cupid was daydreaming about Dexter Charming. She could hardly believe it when he sat down next to her. He'd found a forbidden book: *The History of True Hearts Day*. He told Cupid all about it.

"*Shhh!*" hissed the step-librarians.

Cupid asked Headmaster Grimm if Ever After High could spellebrate True Hearts Day, which invited everyone to follow their true heart's desire.

"That holiday is dangerous!" exclaimed Headmaster Grimm. He wanted students to follow their destinies— not their heart's desires!

But Cupid and her friend Briar Beauty decided to throw a top-secret True Hearts Day dance. Briar was a spelltacular party planner.

"It will be happily ever awesome!" said Cupid.

Briar was thrilled to begin party planning! She had decorations and refreshments to order. She just had to make sure that Headmaster Grimm didn't find out what they were doing.

Hearts and destinies don't always move in the same direction. Ashlynn Ella, daughter of Cinderella, and Hunter Huntsman, son of the Huntsman, were not in the same fairytale. They weren't supposed to live Happily Ever After together. But they were having a lovely picnic in the Enchanted Forest.

Duchess Swan and Sparrow Hood discovered them!

"You two are totally busted!" sang Sparrow, strumming on his guitar.

"Please," begged Ashlynn. "You can't tell anyone Hunter and I are dating."

But Duchess refused to keep their secret.

Cupid was broadcasting her MirrorCast about love.

"Fragile in fairyland, what's in your heart?" she asked.

Dexter Charming phoned in, pretending to be someone else. "I have a crush on Raven Queen. But whenever I'm around her, I'm tongue-tied."

Cupid realized who was calling. She was disappointed that Dexter didn't have a crush on her, too. But it was her destiny to help everyone find love! She advised him to put down his thoughts on parchment.

So Dexter left Raven a poem at her locker signed "D. Charming." Just as Raven was reading it, Dexter's brother, Daring, passed by. Raven thought the love note was from him!

The path of true love isn't always perfectly clear.

Ashlynn was shopping for shoes with Apple White. She wanted to tell her best friend forever after that she was dating Hunter—but she couldn't.

Instead, she asked for advice from Cedar Wood. "Duchess is going to spell it out for the whole school. What should I do?"

The daughter of Pinocchio always told the truth—she had to. Cedar touched her nose. "I think it's better not to lie."

Headmaster Grimm caught Cupid, Briar, and Hopper Croakington II carrying a box of heart-shaped cakes. He was suspicious. Were they planning a party? But they told him they were props for a play.

"What's the name of this play?" asked the headmaster.

"The Play That Almost Was but Then Wasn't," Hopper said sheepishly.

Duchess wanted Blondie Lockes, Ever After High's top reporter, to spill the magic beans about Ashlynn. But she didn't have to! Ashlynn and Hunter told the whole school that they were dating.

Duchess was royally upset!

Apple White was confused by the news, because she believed in following your destiny.

Raven thought it was hexcellent that Ashlynn and Hunter were rewriting their destinies. But Apple was worried. If characters didn't follow their destinies, their books could close forever!

Duchess approached Ashlynn to tell her that she was doing the right thing—and this made Ashlynn worry. Her best friend was upset by what she was doing, yet Duchess approved. Was she making the wrong decision?

Ashlynn went to the Castleteria and told Hunter they needed to talk. "I think we should break up," she told him.

Hunter was heartbroken.

The sun was setting. Students were getting ready for the big, secret True Hearts Day dance. There were gowns to slip on, ribbons to tie, crowns to polish, and glass slippers to put on. One by one, the students snuck out their windows to head to the dance.

Sparrow was jamming on his guitar when Duchess found him. She needed his help to find out where the dance was being held—and to ruin it!

"If Briar gets in trouble, there will be a new opening in the royal ranks," she told him.

But Sparrow didn't want to help Duchess. He also hadn't gotten an invitation to the dance…because he was friends with Duchess.

How could Duchess find out where the dance was happening? Then it hit her! There was one person who was cursed to tell the truth, and that was Cedar Wood.

Once she knew the party location, Duchess danced over to Headmaster Grimm's office to tell him the news! She couldn't wait to ruin the dance for everyone, and to get Briar in trouble.

The music was blaring. Strobe lights flashed across the dance floor. Melody Piper, the Pied Piper's daughter, was the DJ, and her music had everyone dancing.

Except for Ashlynn. She was trying to avoid Hunter. She felt terrible about breaking up with him.

Duchess led Headmaster Grimm through the woods, following the sound of the music. The headmaster kicked down the door—and surprised Sparrow, who was practicing with his band, the Merry Men. This wasn't a secret dance! He gave Duchess detention.

Had Cedar lied to Duchess? No! Her friends had told her the wrong information—so Duchess wouldn't find out what was going on. But they made sure to bring Cedar to the party themselves.

Raven noticed Daring Charming bragging to a group of girls. She thanked him for the poem, but he had no idea what she was talking about.

D. Charming. Dexter, Raven realized. The shy prince.

Dexter saw his brother talking to Raven and he was sad.
"Why does my brother always get the girl?" he asked Cupid.
"Stop thinking so much about your brother and think
about yourself. You are great just the way you are.
Cross my heart," she told him.
"Thanks, Cupid!" He placed his hand over hers.
That's when Raven spotted him—and it looked to
her like he was holding hands with Cupid.
She was too late.

Cupid took the stage. She wanted to share the legend of True Hearts Day with everyone.

"Once upon a time, there grew a heart tree. Even if the winter was harsh, the heart tree blossomed, no matter what. Our fairytale ancestors gave the blossoms to one another on True Hearts Day. True love will always find a way. Follow your true heart."

Fairies flew into the room, each one carrying a special heart for every guest. Ashlynn held hers in her hand. She knew who it belonged to. She gave her heart to Hunter. Everyone applauded.

Even Apple. "I might worry about you," she told her friend, "but I want you to know that we'll always be friends, no matter what. That's what's in my true heart." She gave her special heart to her best friend forever after—Ashlynn.

"I'm going to do it. I'm going to do it," said Dexter, summoning his courage. He wanted to give his heart to Raven. But before he could, Madeline Hatter pulled her on the dance floor, and Lizzie snatched the heart out of his hands.

Too late!

Well, there was always next year's True Hearts Day. Some princes had to wait a long time to find their destiny!